In memory of Louisa (the real Miranda!)

Contents

Chapter 1
Sleep? No chance!

Is my dad crazy?!

I mean, sometimes he really acts like it.

"What's up, Dixie?" my dad asks, as he puts his head round the door of my bedroom. "Can't sleep? Need Daddy to read you a story?"

Yeah, *right* ...

Dad has to be crazy. And this is why.

First of all, I'm thirteen, and no one reads me stories in bed any more.

Also, he's nuts if he thinks it's funny to joke around at a time like this. (But, you know, he's *always* joking around.)

I mean, how can I ever fall asleep tonight, when tomorrow will be THE most exciting day of my life so far?

As Dad stands there grinning, I feel like I might throw something at him.

But then in my hands is the latest *Candy* magazine, and that's *way* too special to chuck at Dad's head!

Luckily, he plods off – but then it's Mum's turn.

"Dixie, you've really got to get some sleep," she says.

"But I need to read this. I'm doing research!" I tell her. I've flipped *Candy* magazine open at *'Share it with Sharron'*, the page where readers write in with their problems.

Sharron Ford is the problem page editor. She looks so warm and friendly in her photo. You feel like you could tell her *anything* and she'd make it OK.

Wow, I can't *wait* to meet her for real …

"Dixie, do I have to come and *make* you stop reading?" Mum says in a cross voice but I know she's not really mad at me. She's the same as Dad – she likes joking around.

I giggle, and make like I'm snuggling down, just to please her.

Mum goes, but I'm not left alone for long.

"You're *texting* under there, aren't you?" I suddenly hear my big sister Tess say.

I can't hear her very well, but that's 'cos I'm under my duvet. And I have to reply to my friend Ella's good luck message.

All Ella's written is *"U R SOOOOOOOOOO LUCKY!!!!!"*, but I get what she means.

I peep out from under the duvet. "No," I lie.

"Dixie, I can *hear* all the clicking!" says Tess and she pulls the duvet off me with a *whoosh*.

"I'm just finishing!" I moan.

"No, you're not," she snaps and she grabs my phone off me. "You promised Mum that you'd go to sleep, and you haven't. So I'm taking *this*."

"Tess! Give that *back*!" I shout after her, but she's already gone.

In case you haven't worked it out yet, Tess is *nothing* like me and our mum and dad. She *never* likes to goof around.

Here's what Tess likes to do:

1) be serious

2) work all the time

3) have a go at me when I get one of my giggling fits.

But here's something that me and Tess both do have in common – we *both* read *Candy* magazine.

And here's something *else* I'm pretty sure of – Tess is *jealous* of me.

But *I* can't help it if I'm chatty. And how is it my fault that I was chatting to our new neighbour Rachel who works in the same office block as *Candy* magazine?

And I can't help it if Rachel got me some work experience at *Candy* for this half-term.

The thing is, I feel totally sunshine-y inside, and I'm not going to let my sister act like a big, fat rain cloud and spoil all my fun.

'Cos *Candy*, here I come!

Chapter 2
OK, take a deep breath ...

"How are you feeling?" asks my neighbour Rachel.

"I'm fine!" I lie, but my heart is banging so hard I'm sure that everyone in the lift can hear it.

Then *shooom*, the shiny metal doors of the lift glide open, and right in front of me is a huge poster with big pink lettering on it.

It says 'Shout if you want Candy!'.

I'm so excited I nearly yell '**Yes please!**'.

Lucky I don't yell for real, 'cos someone's just come to meet me and she *might* think I'm crazy and tell me to go home.

"Are you ditzy?" she asks as she looks me up and down.

That's a bit rude.

"*Dixie!*" Rachel laughs. "Her name's Dixie!"

The girl doesn't look much older than Tess. She gives a shrug.

"OK, *Dixie*," she says and gets it right this time. "My name's Miranda, and I'm the Editor's Assistant here at *Candy*. Follow me."

I say bye-bye to Rachel, and follow Miranda into the *Candy* office. She pushes open a swish-looking door and we walk in.

I'm so excited I feel sick and I worry for a second that I might really throw up.

How would that look? I don't think Sharron Ford and the rest of the cool *Candy* staff would like that much?!

But I'm OK and I look round and see a big, bright room ... which is totally *empty*!

I don't know what I thought the *Candy* office would be like. Maybe full of chatter and laughter, with some of the staff giving me a friendly wave hello?

Miranda turns and sees me staring at the empty desks and computers.

"Everyone's in a meeting with the Editor," she says. She points out a small office with glass walls. There's ten people crammed in there. They've all got note-pads and they're writing stuff down. I know who the Editor is. I remember her name. It's cute and she writes a letter at the beginning of the magazine every week. "Is that Polly Cheer?" I ask.

"Yes, that's right," Miranda says. "But now I'm going to show you who your best friend for the week is!"

Is this where I get to meet Sharron Ford? I think. Fingers crossed …

Er, no.

Miranda's pointing at a *kettle*.

A kettle which is sitting on a work-top, with a stack of dirty cups all round it.

I think Miranda spots the puzzled look on my face.

"The kettle will be your best friend, because you'll be making tea and coffee for

everyone. *Lots* of it. *All* day," she tells me.
"That's basically your job while you're here."

"Um, OK," I mutter. The news is a bit of a
let down.

But I suppose there is *one* person who I'd
be happy to make *endless* cups of tea for, if it
means I can hang out and chat with her.

"Is, er, Sharron Ford in that meeting too?"
I ask as I scan all the faces in the Editor's
office.

"Nope. She phoned in sick today," says
Miranda, as she hands me a pen and a note-
pad.

Hey, it's like a proper reporter's note-pad!

Maybe that was a joke about making tea
all day!

Maybe Miranda wants me to interview someone famous first!

"Go on," she says, and points me towards Polly Cheer's office.

"Really?" I gasp. Am I really going into that important meeting with the Editor so soon?

"Yep," says Miranda with a nod. "Just make a list of who wants tea and who wants coffee. And don't forget to ask who has sugar!"

Hmmm.

Maybe life at *Candy* magazine isn't quite as cool as I'd expected.

At least not for *me* …

Chapter 3
Not as great as all that

"So are they all really nice?" asks Mum as she puts a big heap of pasta on my plate.

Phew – I'm starving.

I felt so nervous at lunch time that all I ate was a corner of my peanut butter sandwich, as I sat on my own at my desk, flicking through old copies of *Candy*.

"Mmm, yes," I answer as if I'm not really listening.

I mean, the staff of *Candy* <u>might</u> be the nicest, friendliest people in the world, but they all seemed WAY too busy to be nice or friendly to *me* today.

"So have they asked you to be the new Editor yet?" Dad jokes.

Mum goes as if to hit him on the head with the serving spoon.

"Just ignore him, Dixie," she laughs. "Go on – tell us more!"

"Um … well, on Wednesday, there's going to be a photo-shoot for the next front cover of the magazine," I tell them. I heard some people talking about it.

"Oooh!" says Mum, as Dad makes a 'surprised' face.

"Then there's the *Candy* Fun Day on Friday," I carry on. "Zack McCloud will be there!"

Two hundred lucky readers won tickets to the *Candy* Fun Day. It's a once-a-year party with give-aways and on-the-spot makeovers and there'll be some celebrities there too.

Me and my friend Ella tried to win tickets but we didn't make it.

"Zack McCloud? *Really?*" gasps Mum, and she sounds very impressed.

Dad frowns and I can see he's thinking hard. "Is he an actor in that Australian soap you and Tess like?"

"Yeah," I say. Tess doesn't really watch it any more – she's too busy with all her important course-work for that.

In fact, she makes me feel *dumb* for chatting about my favourite TV shows.

"Wow ... Zack McCloud. Did you hear that, Tess?" asks Mum and looks over at my sister.

"Yeah, whatever," Tess mutters. She doesn't even look up.

To me, that sounds like she's jealous for sure – or just being *mean*.

Y'know, I *had* been about to admit that my day hadn't been all that great.

But now, no *way* will I let Tess know that *Candy* isn't so sweet ...

Chapter 4
What's the problem?

On Tuesday morning, I make my way shyly into the *Candy* office.

"OK, Dixie," says Miranda, "I've got something *different* for you to do today ..."

Oh, thank goodness!

I made so many cups of tea and coffee yesterday that I spent all last night dreaming that giant tea bags were chasing me round the *Candy* office.

"Here you are ..." Miranda goes on and kicks at a massive grey post sack with the toe of her shoe. "Problem page letters for Sharron."

My heart misses a beat.

"Oh! Is Sharron ..." I begin.

"Nope, she's not coming in today either," Miranda says quickly, 'cos she knows what I'm about to ask. "Anyway, just sort all the letters into different piles … *'I'm Being Bullied'; 'Does He Fancy Me?'; 'Am I A Freak?'* – that sort of thing."

That's a much better job than making tea but at the same time I'm shocked.

What about all those girls who've sat and told Sharron all their deepest secrets and fears?

Won't they feel gutted if they know it's *me* – thirteen-year-old *Dixie* – reading all their private problems?!

"And once you've done that," Miranda says, "you need to choose three that you think could be the top letters for next week's *'Share it with Sharron'* page."

"You want *me* to choose?!" I squeak in surprise.

"Yep," says Miranda, as she walks off.

Help!

I mean, I love *'Share it with Sharron'*, but this feels like I'm being seriously *nosey* ...

But it beats making a million cups of tea and coffee.

And so I pull out my first handful of letters.

And then another.

And another.

And *another*.

Until suddenly it's early afternoon, and my head is swirling with sad and sometimes scary stories from other people's lives.

"Picked your three problems yet?" asks Miranda as she gets back from lunch.

"Well, I've chosen these ..." I answer. I show her three letters I've put on the desk.

They are:

♡ *'My Boobs Are Too Small!'* (I like this one 'cos most of my friends worry that their chest is too small, or too big, or just not the same as everyone else's.)

♡ *'Why Has He Changed?'* (This girl doesn't understand why this boy's suddenly stopped being nice to her. I want to know what Sharron will say 'cos I don't understand boys either.)

♡ *'Help, I Can't Take the Stress!'* (From someone whose mum and dad are pressuring her into doing lots of exams. *My* mum and dad are so laid-back that I feel really sorry for this girl.)

"OK," says Miranda with a shrug. She doesn't even look at the letters. "Now, how about getting the kettle on?"

Sigh.

When my neighbour Rachel asked me if I wanted to do some work experience in the *Candy* office, I thought it would be *amazing*.

I thought I might meet models and pop stars and celebrities.

I didn't expect to be the office *slave*.

There's hardly any point in me being here – I might as well be spending my half-term with Ella, hanging out in our bedrooms.

"Oh, by the way," Miranda says suddenly, "can Rachel bring you into the office a little bit earlier tomorrow? We'll be leaving for the photo-shoot at 9am sharp."

"The photo-shoot for the next front cover?" I squeak. "You mean, *I* can *come?*"

"Of course!" says Miranda with a laugh.

"*YESSS!*" I squeak again.

Y'know, with all this squeaking, Miranda must think I'm half-girl, half-*mouse* ...

Chapter 5
Giggling and grumbles

It's Tuesday evening, and my best friend Ella has come around to mine for a gossip.

"I wonder what the model will be like?" says Ella, as she swaps CDs in my player.

She's almost as excited as *I* am about tomorrow's photo-shoot – she's even let me borrow her coolest top.

"Well, we all know the model won't be *nearly* as gorgeous as *me*!" I say, joking around as I look at myself in the mirror and try on Ella's shiny black shirt.

"*Or* me!" laughs Ella, and turns the music up loud.

Next thing, we're both making faces in the mirror and doing swanky cat-walk moves.

Then we burst into cackles of laughter.

"Would you two give me a break?" a voice suddenly grumbles loudly.

Me and Ella both spin round and see Tess standing at my door.

Her face is like thunder.

Honestly, you'd think we'd done something terrible, like super-glued her textbooks shut.

"We were only ..." I start to say.

But I don't get very far.

"Who cares *what* you were doing? I just wish you wouldn't do it so *loud*!" Tess snaps. "How am I supposed to get any studying done?"

Ella and I stay statue still. There's no point in arguing.

"What's up with *her*?" Ella whispers when Tess has stomped back to her own room.

"I think a wicked witch put a spell on my nice sister and turned her into a total grouch queen," I joke.

Though deep down, I feel kind of sorry and sad that Tess doesn't seem to know how much fun, well, *fun* is ...

Chapter 6

Looking good!
(Sounding bad ...)

Normally at 9.30am on a Wednesday, I'm in Mr Williams' Physics class.

But at 9.30am *this* Wednesday, I'm in a fancy photographer's studio with spot-lights and cameras, along with the Editor AND the Fashion Editor of *Candy* magazine.

How amazing is that?

But I have to say, *getting* here wasn't all that amazing.

At 9am, Polly Cheer (the Editor) and Amy Flint (the Fashion Editor) slunk into a waiting black cab with bags and bags of clothes to take to the photo-shoot.

At 9.01am, Miranda and me *walked* to the photographer's studio, carrying the four bags that hadn't fitted in the black cab.

Wow, my arms hurt.

But it was all worth it once we got into the studio. It was enormous and really cool!

I felt all fluttery and excited inside – even if Polly Cheer the Editor was the exact *opposite* of cheerful (one of the models hadn't turned up yet).

And I still felt all fluttery and excited, even when Miranda told me *why* I'd been asked along today.

Oh, yes – I was there to make *endless* cups of tea for everyone.

And, it turns out, for someone called *Calum*.

"D–d–do you take sugar?" I ask now, my voice is a bit wobbly.

That's because I'm looking into the eyes of a very gorgeous male model (Calum).

He's about eighteen, has floppy brown hair, and is so handsome that it's making me dizzy.

"Two," he says as he checks out how he looks in the mirror.

I can't stop staring at him and I nearly trip over Miranda as I back out of the dressing room.

"I thought there was just going to be a *girl* model!" I whisper to her.

"Polly the Editor wants a cute, romantic cover for the next issue of *Candy*," Miranda says. "So Amy booked a girl *and* a boy. But if the girl doesn't turn up soon, maybe they'll have to get *you* to stand in for her!"

I'm glad she didn't tell me that when I was carrying a tray of teas and coffees. They'd be spilt all over the floor by now, 'cos I've gone so wibbly thinking about snuggling up to Calum!

"OK, panic over – here she is now," Miranda says, as a tall, pretty girl comes hurrying in, carrying a bottle of water and telling us all how she got stuck in traffic.

Before the model gets a chance to breathe, Amy the Fashion Editor walks her to the dressing room, where three things are waiting for her:

1) some great clothes to wear

2) a make-up artist to make her even
more lovely, and ...

3) Calum, of course!

Lucky her.

Still, I'm feeling pretty lucky myself
today.

After two days of feeling that my work
experience isn't that great, this is *much*
more exciting, and just how I thought life at
a magazine would be.

The only thing that would be more of a
thrill is if I could meet Sharron Ford at last ...

"So are you looking forward to the *Candy
Fun Day* on Friday?" Miranda says with a
grin, as she helps me by getting some cups
out of a cupboard.

I'm so surprised the water goes all over my hand instead of into the kettle.

"You mean, *I* get to go to that *too*?" I squeak (as normal).

Today can't really get much better for me!

But it suddenly sounds as if it's not going very well for someone *else* ...

I spin round to see Calum and the girl model having a full-on, stand-up yelling match.

And – ooof! – the girl has just poured her bottle of water over his *head*!

Well, it doesn't look like they're in the mood to cuddle up for a romantic photo-shoot ...

Chapter 7
Spilling the gossip

I tell Mum and Dad and Ella all about what happened at the photo shoot when I get home. "It turns out," I say, "that Calum and the girl model used to be *boyfriend* and *girlfriend*. They only split up last week."

I know Tess is listening too, but she's pretending to read one of her text-books.

"Uh-oh!" says Ella, who's come around to hear all today's gossip.

"Wonder what the lad did to annoy her?" laughs Dad.

"Oh, dear – didn't they know they'd *both* been booked for the same magazine photo-shoot?" Mum asks.

"I guess not ..." I reply. I remember Calum and the girl's pretend smiles when the photographer started snapping at last.

Oh, yes – the models *had* to do their job in the end.

But it took *ages* for the Fashion Editor to cool everyone down.

Then Calum had to change out of his wet clothes and get his floppy hair blow-dried.

And, the make-up artist had a very tricky job to make the girl model look like she *hadn't* been sobbing her eyes out.

"Check *this*," I say and I take one of the photographer's left over photos from my pocket.

Mum, Dad and Ella bunch together right away to gawp at the photo.

(Out of the corner of my eye, I spot Tess twitch – I know she's dying to peek but she's too stubborn to show she's interested.)

"Ooh!" Mum says. "That poor girl's eyes are so red that it looks like she's had a bucket of sand kicked in them!"

"And I think I'd call that *snarling* more than smiling!" Dad jokes.

As my parents and Ella study the picture, I remember my good news.

"Hey, guess what? I got told that I can go to the *Candy* Fun Day on Friday, AND I can bring a friend!"

"You mean ... *me?*" says Ella, in a voice as squeaky as mine has been all week.

"Of *course*, you!" I giggle. I spot Tess shutting her text-book and stomping away.

Why does she always have to go and spoil my good news by being a total *grump?*

Chapter 8
A not-so-nice surprise

Oh.

It's Thursday morning, and I've just walked into the *Candy* office but there's a woman sitting at my desk.

She has grey streaks in her hair and she's eating a doughnut.

I shouldn't be mean, but she looks like she eats a *lot* of doughnuts.

"Um, hello," I say shyly. "That's where, *I've*, um, been sitting the last few days ..."

"Are you Claire? Or Vicky?" says the woman and sugar sprinkles and crumbs drop all over the neat pile of problem page letters I've been sorting.

"My name's Dixie," I answer her. *What's she getting at?* I ask myself.

"Well, I always muddle up all you work experience girls," the woman says. "So I see you've chosen something for my page ..."

As the woman reads the three letters on the desk that I pulled out of the post-bag early in the week, I gasp, "Are ... are you *Sharron Ford?*"

"Uh-huh!" answers the woman, not looking at me. "Now can you put them onto the computer, and write answers for them? About fifty words for each will do."

"Huh? But I–I don't know if ... I–I mean – " I start to splutter.

"Do what you can. I'll read them and fix them up afterwards."

With that, Sharron Ford gets up and goes towards Polly the Editor's office with her doughnut.

Help! I don't know what to do – except do as I'm told, I guess ...

With shaking hands, I pick up a letter.

It's the one about being stressed.

It says:

'Dear Sharron –

My parents expect me to do really well at school, but I'm not as smart as they think I am and it's getting really difficult. I work so hard, I never get to have a good time any more. I feel so down – what can I do?

Candy Girl'

But I don't have a clue what to say, because I'm still too stunned, AND because I'm only thirteen and not a problem page expert!

"What's up?" I hear Miranda ask.

She sits on the edge of my desk, and looks at me.

"I just met Sharron Ford," I say. It's like I've just seen a ghost.

"Oh, yeah?" smirks Miranda. "And what do you think?"

"Well, she doesn't look much like her *photo*!" I blurt out. The Sharron Ford in the photo on her problem page is a slim, blonde young woman with a great big smile.

"I guess she did look like that once, only it must have been *years* ago," says Miranda, with a cheeky grin.

I don't have time to think about how Sharron fools *Candy* readers with her out-of-date photo, 'cos I need to tell Miranda something *else*.

"*And* she's asked me to write answers to the problems she's been sent!"

"Oh, yeah – she *always* does that," says Miranda with a shrug. "If there isn't a work experience girl like you around, she expects *me* to write it."

"But it's her job! Why doesn't she answer girls' letters herself?" I ask.

"Um, because she's really lazy?" hints Miranda.

And right then, I know that Miranda doesn't think that much of Sharron Ford.

Now I remember how she pulled a face at the start of the week, when she told me that Sharron had phoned in sick.

"Maybe *I* should write a letter to the problem page," Miranda suddenly says with a laugh. "'*Dear Sharron, I work with someone who is lazy and expects everyone else to do her work for her!*' How would that be? Ha ha ha!"

As Miranda walks away, I think of the things that I didn't expect at *Candy* ...

1) the staff who treat me as if they can't see me, like I'm invisible

2) the fact that I'm the tea slave

3) getting to see that Polly Cheer the Editor is mostly grumpy

4) and that Sharron Ford isn't the warm, you-can-tell-me-anything big sister sort of person I thought she'd be.

Well, hurray for the *Candy* Fun Day tomorrow – at least *that'll* be a brilliant laugh, specially since I'll have Ella to hang out with.

I can't *wait*!

Chapter 9
Ella's no-show

"Hello, Dixie! Did you get Ella's message?" asks Mum, as soon as I'm back home.

"Uh, no," I reply and plonk my bag on the kitchen table to look for my mobile.

As soon as I take it out, I see it's got no battery.

"Ella did try to ring you," Dad says. "It turns out, she can't come with you to the Fun Day thing."

"Yeah, *right!*" I laugh back at him. I can always spot one of his wind-ups a mile off.

There's no *way* Ella would miss the *Candy* magazine party, OR miss the chance to gawp at a celebrity like Zack McCloud.

"He's not joking," Tess butts in. She looks up from the table where her text-books are all around her – as ever. "I took her call."

"It's 'cos of *The Lion King*," says Dad. He's trying to tell me why, but I'm getting even more puzzled.

"Ella forgot that her aunt is coming to take her to see *The Lion King* at the theatre tomorrow," Mum joins in. I'm beginning to get it now.

I feel a sudden rush of *total* let down.

"But – but couldn't they swap the tickets for a different day?" I suggest in a panic, looking from Mum to Dad as if they could change things.

I don't look at Tess, 'cos I have the feeling she might just be smirking.

"Well, *no*, Dixie," says Mum. "Ella said that her aunt has taken time off work specially."

"How about one of your *other* friends?" Dad asks.

I'm about to tell him that they're all away on holiday, but stop – because I suddenly realise I'm going to *cry*.

I bet my grumpy, no-fun sister will be *pleased* to see me as sad as her, but I run out of the room before she can see my tears.

"Dixie?" Mum's voice says softly, a few minutes later, at my bedroom door. "I've just had a really good idea!"

I peek out from under my pillow, and listen to what she has to say.

And you know what?

It's the *worst* idea EVER!

Chapter 10
The party

The BEST thing about the *Candy* Fun Day – I don't have to make tea for anyone!

(We're in a club, and the bar is serving fruit cocktails with curly straws in.)

The WORST thing about the *Candy* Fun Day – Tess is standing right next to me.

Yes, you heard right!

I really didn't want to invite my sister along, but Mum said Tess was working so hard all the time that she needed a treat.

Huh!

But in the end, Mum looked at me with such begging puppy-dog eyes that I had to say OK, didn't I?

It's weird, I've just spent the last half-hour alone with my sister – who I'd never hang out with even for five *minutes* at home.

Not that we've done much talking – it's been mostly looking.

We've walked about in the crowds of competition winners, then checked out the different stands. There's an Instant Makeover Stand, a Nail Bar and somewhere you can get Henna Tattoos.

We've seen a zillion girls screaming and crowding round Zack McCloud. All they want is his autograph and to get their photos taken with him.

We've peeked in a sound-proofed room, where you get filmed shouting "I want *Candy*!" as loud as you can.

(After a week at *Candy*, I didn't feel much like shouting that. And the only shouting Tess ever does is at *me*, yelling at me to shut up ...)

Tess and I have got special staff wristbands. So now we've gone back-stage to see what's happening there. A frosty-looking Polly Cheer is in some sort of growly argument with Miranda.

"That's the Editor and her assistant," I whisper to Tess. I can't work out what's going on.

I don't have to wait long to find out.

"Wow, *she's* in a bad mood!" Miranda mutters, as Polly stomps off onto the stage. Right away Polly sticks on a bright grin as she faces about two hundred very excited *Candy* readers.

"What was all that about?" I ask Miranda. She's standing with a sticky roller thing in her hand.

"She told me I hadn't de-fluffed her dress," says Miranda, holding up the roller.

"Is that part of your *job*?" Tess asks in surprise.

"Only until next week. Then I'm going to university to train to be a nurse."

"You're leaving *Candy*?" I squeak in surprise.

I bet every girl in this club today would think Miranda had their absolute *dream* job.

"Yep," Miranda answers. "I'm fed up of all the phonies and fakes I meet!"

Phonies and fakes ... I guess I'd seen a lot of that this week.

♡ A magazine that's super-friendly to read, with totally *unfriendly* staff.

♡ An Editor who scowls close up and then smiles in the spotlight.

♡ Models who can't stand each other but pretend to be loved up.

♡ Problem page editors who don't *care*.

No wonder Miranda wants to ditch all that to do some good!

"Oi, you! Hold this junk!" a bossy Australian voice suddenly booms at Tess.

I turn my head to see the one and only Zack McCloud. He shoves a load of single red roses, two teddy bears and a bunch of hand-made cards into Tess's arms.

Then – just like Polly Cheer – his scowl switches into a smile as he walks on the stage and waves at his fans. What would they say if they knew he'd just dumped all the flowers and cards they gave him?

Tess turns and stares at me and Miranda, her mouth open in shock because ...

a) she was so close to a celebrity, and

b) he was so rude!

And then she does something weird – she bursts out laughing ...

For a second I just stare at her.

I mean, hearing Tess laugh is like hearing a cat quack.

But it does shake up a memory in my mind of a time when Tess *used* to laugh.

When did she stop? When did Tess turn into a no-fun, human rain-cloud?

"Just dump that stuff over there," Miranda tells Tess and points at some tables laid out with nibbles.

I follow Tess over, mainly 'cos I've just spotted someone I want to tell her about.

Someone who's standing by the tables hoovering up all the food as if she hasn't eaten for a week.

"You'll never guess who *that* is!" I whisper in Tess's ear.

"Who?" she whispers back, an excited smile on her face.

"Sharron Ford!" I tell her.

Tess stops dead. She stops giggling.

All the teddies, flowers and cards fall out of her arms and onto the floor.

Wow, *that* was a weird way to react!

"She doesn't look much like her photo, does she?" I say as I bend down to help Tess grab the stuff up again.

"It's not *that*," Tess says, with a shake of her head.

Her hands are trembling.

"Well, what is it?" I ask her back.

"I sent a letter to her problem page a few weeks ago," Tess admits.

"You did?" I squeak.

Tess is super-smart, has a bunch of good mates and a pretty nice family – so what problems could she have?

"Yeah ... it's just that ... well, I *hate* sixth form!" Tess says. "The work is *way* too hard!"

"Oh! Have you told Mum and Dad that?" I ask.

"I don't want to ... they're always going on about how proud they are of me being so smart. I can't let them down, Dixie!"

Wait a minute! Could my moaning grouch queen of a sister be 'Candy Girl'? I think to myself. I remember the three letters I chose for the *'Share it with Sharron'* page.

"Tess – did you use your own name when you wrote your letter?" I ask slowly.

"No ... I knew you read that page and didn't want you to know it was me," Tess answers as she goes on staring over at Sharron Ford. "So I called myself *'Candy Girl'*. Do you think Sharron's read it yet? And what will she tell me?"

I know the answer to *both* those questions.

But Tess doesn't need to know that Sharron hasn't even bothered to look at her letter yet.

But, I *can* tell her what the reply is, 'cos *I* wrote it!

Chapter 11
Sweet enough

"Here it is!" says Tess and holds open the latest *Candy* magazine.

She reads out a reply on the *'Share it with Sharron'* page.

Dear Candy Girl,

You feel stressed out about doing well at school, but you know what? Your parents will be upset to know that you're so down. Tell them that you're finding things tough at the moment. You'll be so glad you did, I promise!

Sharron xxx

Tess turns and gives me a smile. "Sharron didn't change a word of what you wrote, Dixie!" she says proudly.

It's been a week since the *Candy* Fun Day, and here's what's happened since:

⬭   I (the dumb little sister) made Tess (the smart big sister) tell Mum and Dad how she was feeling.

💗   Our parents set up a meeting with Tess and her form teacher, to work out how to make things easier for her at school.

💗   Mum and Dad made a new rule – to have a Family Fun Day once a week (we're all on our way to the cinema right now).

"Hey, guess what, girls?" says Dad, as me and Tess come out of the paper shop with *Candy* magazine in our hands. "Mum and I have changed our minds about going to see that movie. We thought you might like to go to the DIY store instead!"

Dad's lame joke gets a groan from me.

It gets a slap on the shoulder from Tess, with the rolled-up copy of *Candy*.

"Ow!" yelps Dad as if it really hurt.

And now that Tess has read what she wanted to read (and used the mag on Dad!), she goes and drops it in the nearest bin.

"Oh! Don't you *want* that, Dixie?" Mum asks me with a frown.

"Nope," I reply with a grin, hooking my arm into Tess's.

The truth is, I don't want *Candy* any more

'Cos life is sweet enough as it is ...

AUTHOR ID

Name: Karen McCombie

Likes: Crisps and dancing.

Dislikes: Moaners (boo!)

3 words that best describe me:
Chatty but shy.

A secret not many people know:
My guilty pleasure is a bowl of Brussels sprouts
(mmm...)

ILLUSTRATOR ID

Name: Jessica Secheret

Likes: Massage, chocolate and my
baby girl!

Dislikes: Insects.

3 words that best describe me: Optimistic,
dynamic and curious.

A secret not many people know: I have a
tattoo somewhere.

Barrington Stoke would like to thank all its readers for commenting on the manuscript before publication and in particular:

Izu Akwari
Edouard Baliu
Néve Barker
Emma Carl
Maddie Curran
Holly Dayson
Tori Kate Fleet
Sarah Fleet
Dhaval Gajre
Kerry Hodges
Luci Hodges
Lemonia Koutsabeloulis
Bianca McKay

Jessica Nimmo
Isaac Davies Oliveck
Melissa Davies Oliveck
William Olbrys
Onur Ozsayan
Alex Pearson
Xian Pelaez
Vaadet Raim
Ben Sintim
Dee Dexter Smith
Hannah Smith
Kim Stone
Sara Ward

Become a Consultant!

Would you like to be a consultant? Ask your parent, carer or teacher to contact us at the email address below – we'd love to hear from them! They can also find out more by visiting our website.

schools@barringtonstoke.co.uk
www.barringtonstoke.co.uk

The Sticky Witch
by
Hilary McKay

Tom and Ellie (and Whiskers the Cat) have to go and live with Aunt Tab.
That's bad.
Everything in her house is sticky with treacle.
That's worse.
Then they find out she's a witch.
Will Tom and Ellie come to a sticky end?

Desirable
by
Frank Cottrell Boyce

George is a loser. Then he starts using the aftershave that he got for his birthday. Suddenly all the girls are in love with him ... and that includes the teachers! George wanted to be popular. Now he's looking for somewhere to hide ...

You can order these books directly from our website at
www.barringtonstoke.co.uk

The Story of Matthew Buzzington
by
Andy Stanton

Who on Earth is Matthew Buzzington? I hear you ask. Well, he's just a normal 10-year-old boy. But ... Matthew Buzzington can turn into a fly.
Imagine that! It's just that, well, he hasn't yet. But he'll need to soon to beat the bully out to get him ...

Zack Black and the Magic Dads
by
Annie Dalton

Zack doesn't need a dad, but his mum thinks he does. The Magic Dad website seems like the way to make her happy. But it's not that easy. With each new Magic Dad, things go from bad to worse! Can Zack find a new dad – or is he looking in all the wrong places?

You can order these books directly from our website at www.barringtonstoke.co.uk